To
the great kids of Newburyport,

When you get hungry, our
family recommends . . . . .

2 Breads Like A Sandwich!

-GABE-

Two Breads
Like a Sandwich

Dedicated to the three ladies
I'm lucky enough to live with—
Joanna, Jilly, and Ellie

Manufactured by Regent Publishing Services Ltd Printed October 2021
in Shenzhen, China

Hardcover ISBN: 978-1-938394-68-3
Library of Congress Control Number: 2021911285

Great Life Press
Rye, New Hampshire 03870
www.greatlifepress.com

Copies are available from:
The Spicy Shark
www.thespicyshark.com

Two Breads Like a Sandwich

by Gabe DiSaverio

Illustrations by Andreea Togoe

It was snowing in November
A surprise to say the least.
Joanna slept in later than usual
Dreaming of last night's
                Thanksgiving feast.

She heard Papa making coffee downstairs,
But wasn't yet ready to wake.
She closed her eyes for a little bit longer,
Thinking of the cookies Mama had baked.

When Joanna heard Ellie barking,
It was time to get out of bed.
She quickly walked down the stairs
To remind Papa that Ellie needed to be fed.

"Good morning, Banana!" Papa said with a grin.
He was still wearing his pajama pants.
Joanna gave him a big sleepy smile,
And he knew what she wanted in a glance.

"So, tell me about your day, Papa," said Joanna.
"Well, honey it just started, so I'm not sure I can.
How about we have something to eat?"
Joanna perked up, "That sounds like a good plan!"

For breakfast, Joanna usually ate fruit,
Eating grapes and bananas by the ton!
But now that she was four years old,
She had a new obsession.

Ellie started eating her morning meal
And Joanna turned on the last light switch.
"What would you like for breakfast?" Papa asked.
Joanna yelled, "Two breads like a sandwich!"

"Two breads like a sandwich!? You had that yesterday.
How about something different for your belly?"
"Papa, yesterday the breads were with honey.
Today I want peanut butter and jelly."

"Joanna, how about a ripe avocado?"
said Papa as he cleaned out her back pack.
"I'm saving avocado for later," she said.
"I might even have one as a snack."

"How about we start the morning
With a couple of Mama's scones?"
"Papa, I already had three of them
While you were looking at your phone."

"You know Joanna, what could be fun,
Is to make some hard boiled eggs we can store."
"I know that papa, I know," she said,
"But we've already done that before."

"Are you sure you don't want some oatmeal?
Or how about blueberry pancakes!"
"Papa, you're just not listening,
But that's okay, everyone makes mistakes."

"Joanna, we have other food in the fridge.
All the leftovers would still taste fine."
"I really, really want two breads like a sandwich!
Papa, you're wasting my time."

"Okay, two breads like a sandwich, I got it.
Do you want them toasted or plain?"
"As long as there's jelly and peanut butter,
The breads just need to be the same."

Papa spread peanut butter on one bread,
And raspberry jelly on the other.
Joanna started to wiggle and dance,
She couldn't wait very much longer.

Joanna was so happy about breakfast
She let out an eager howl.
"Papa, I'm so very excited!
Please don't forget a paper towel!"

As Joanna ate her breakfast with joy,
Papa had a pretty good hunch
That in less than a couple of hours
She'd want two breads like a sandwich for lunch.

About the Author

After growing up in New Jersey and Long Island, Gabe DiSaverio made Portsmouth, NH his home, where he lives with his wife Jill, daughter Joanna, and Great Dane Ellie. A former bartender and beer salesman, Gabe now runs his family's wedding venue in Norway, Maine, and the award-winning hot sauce company he founded, The Spicy Shark. He loves his family, sharks, and hot sauce.